Estela's Swap

by **ALEXIS O'NEILL**

illustrated by **ENRIQUE O. SANCHEZ**

LEE & LOW BOOKS Inc.

New York

Ballet Folklórico (ba-LEH fo-CLOH-ee-koh): a type of dance group that specializes in Mexican folk dances

bueno (BWEH-noh): good

Cielito Lindo (see-ah-LEE-toe LIN-doh): the name of a song, "Beautiful Heaven"

falda (FAHL-dah): skirt

gracias (GRAH-see-ahs): thank you

Javier (hah-vee-AIR): a boy's name

señora (seh-NYO-rah): Mrs., madame

Manufactured in China by South China Printing Co.

Book design by Christy Hale
Book production by The Kids at Our House

The text is set in Panama Opti
The illustrations are rendered in acrylic on canvas

3 4 5 6 7 8 9 10 HC   PB 10 9 8 7 6 5 4 3 2 1
First Edition

Library of Congress Cataloging-in-Publication Data
O'Neill, Alexis.
Estela's swap / by Alexis O'Neill ; illustrated by Enrique O. Sanchez.— 1st ed.
     p. cm.
Summary: A young Mexican American girl accompanies her father to a swap meet,
where she hopes to sell her music box for money for dancing lessons.
ISBN-13: 978-1-58430-044-1 (hc)   ISBN-13: 978-1-60060-253-5 (pb)
[1. Flea markets—Fiction. 2. Moneymaking projects—Fiction. 3. Music box—Fiction. 4. Conduct
of life—Fiction. 5. Mexican Americans—Fiction.] I. Sanchez, Enrique O., ill. II. Title.
PZ7.O5523 Es 2002   [E]—dc21   2001038785

With love to Donna and Laura.

Thanks, too, to Bob Brown and Mom Boeshaar—A.O.

To Keeko—E.O.S.

Papa's truck bounced through the Swap Meet parking lot early one Sunday in March. Suddenly a strong Santa Ana wind blew a curtain of sand and leaves against the windows. Estela hugged her music box closer.

Her brother, Javier, tugged her braid. "We might have to anchor Estela so she doesn't blow away in the wind today," he teased.

This was the first time Papa had let Estela sell something at Swap Meet. She needed to earn just ten dollars more for folk-dancing lessons in town this summer at the Ballet Folklórico. She had been saving her money all year.

"Come," Papa said. "Let's set up."

From the truck they pulled old toys, clothes, and furniture. They lifted out pots and pans and car parts, and arranged them in their space. Along with their own things, Papa brought anything the neighbors wanted him to sell.

"Here, Estela," said Papa. "You can put your music box on this desk."

"But what if somebody wants to buy the desk?"

Papa laughed. "Then you sell the desk!"

"Bargain with them," Javier said. "Tell them that if they buy the desk, they can have this music box for free."

"I will not, Javier!" Estela replied. "I'll get my price. You wait and see."

"Let's look around," Papa said. "Javier, mind our space while Estela and I are away, please."

Estela picked up her music box.

"Don't take that," Javier called after her. "Someone may want to buy it while you're gone."

Estela pretended not to hear. She wanted to sell her music box herself.

Swap Meet was a little city of tarps and tents and tables. Music blared from several stalls. The aisles buzzed with customers. Delicious smells of hot dogs, chili, and popcorn filled the air.

Papa stopped at one stall and pointed to a hubcap.

"How much?" he asked the man.

"Nine dollars," the man replied.

"I'll give you four," Papa said.

"Sorry," the man answered.

Papa turned away.

Estela tugged at his shirt. "But Papa," she whispered. "We need a hubcap just like that."

"Don't worry," Papa whispered back as he pretended to leave.

All of a sudden the man said, "I'll sell it to you for seven dollars."

"Six dollars," Papa offered. The man agreed.

"See how it's done?" Papa asked as they walked back to their space. "As the seller, you name a price that's a little more than what you are willing to take. That way you have room to bargain. Now it's time for you to try."

Estela set her music box on top of the desk. People walked by without stopping. She opened the cover. The cheerful song *"Cielito Lindo"* began to play.

Across the way a flower seller clapped her hands. *"Bueno!"* she called. A festive tent covered her stall filled with dried flowers in clay pots. Bouquets of tissue paper flowers hung from cords between the tent posts.

Maybe the flower seller is in the mood to buy something, Estela thought. She picked up her music box and walked to the woman's stall.

To pass the time, the flower seller was sewing the hem of a *falda*, a beautiful full skirt with colorful ribbons at the bottom.

Estela imagined how much fun it would be to dance in a skirt just like that. She would twirl around the stage and swirl her skirt like the ocean waves.

"Would you like to see my music box?" Estela asked the flower seller.

The woman's eyes sparkled. "I love this tune," she said. "It reminds me of when I was a little girl."

"I'm selling my music box today," Estela explained. "I need to earn ten more dollars for dancing lessons." Estela tried to keep her feet still, but the song tickled its way to her toes.

The flower seller smiled. "I see you already know some steps." Then she began to hum *Cielito Lindo* as she sewed along the hem of the skirt.

When Estela returned to her side of the aisle, she made sure everyone could hear the music box as they walked by.

A customer paused in front of Estela.

"How much?" he asked.

"Twelve dollars," Estela said. She felt proud that she had left room to bargain.

The man laughed and plunked down the music box. He walked out of sight.

"Do you think he'll be back, Papa?" Estela asked.

"I think he finds your price too high," Papa replied.

A woman stopped next. "Beautiful music!" she said.

"Would you like to make an offer?" Estela asked hopefully.

"Two dollars," the woman said.

Only two dollars? For a moment Estela was speechless. Then she said, "I was asking twelve, but for you . . . I'll sell it to you for ten."

The woman smiled and walked away.

"How's it going?" Javier asked.

"Oh, Javier," Estela said. "I was so sure someone would buy my music box right away."

"Maybe you should've brought more than one thing to sell," Javier said. "Then you'd have more chances to earn ten dollars."

Without warning a strong wind ripped through the Swap Meet, catching everyone by surprise. Tarps tore loose, whipping and snapping. Tents turned topsy-turvy. Dishes crashed and metal poles clanked to the ground. Estela reached for her music box to keep it from blowing away.

"My flowers! My flowers!" the woman across the way called above the clatter. The flower seller's pots had smashed to the ground. Her tissue paper flowers had flown away like birds. She sat on the skirt she was sewing to keep it from flying away too.

Estela ran to help. Without thinking she put her music box on the woman's table. She pulled a tent pole upright so it wouldn't fall on the woman's head. Just then she heard another crash.

Estela spun around.

Her music box! It was smothered by pieces of broken flowerpots.

Oh no! Estela thought. *It's probably broken. No one will buy it now.*

Estela was afraid to look closely. Instead she helped the flower seller. She straightened the tent posts. Then she went up and down the aisles searching for the paper flowers that had blown away.

When Estela returned, the flower seller was smiling. She held out the music box. Estela looked away when she saw its battered cover.

The woman opened the box. The sounds of *"Cielito Lindo"* floated out. "It still sings, little one," the woman said.

Her music box was all right! She could paint over the scratches. She could still sell it.

Estela held her music box tightly and danced for joy. But then she noticed almost everything was gone from the flower seller's stall.

"What will you sell now?" Estela asked.

The woman shook her head. "Today, nothing. But next Sunday—flowers. I have a whole week to make more."

How can she do all that work in just one week? Estela wondered. Suddenly she knew what to do, even if it meant she wouldn't earn any money today.

"Please, *señora*—I want to give you this." Estela held out her music box. "Now you can listen to music while you make flowers."

The flower seller hesitated. Then she said, "*Gracias, little one.*"

Estela walked back across the aisle to where Papa and Javier were waiting. Secretly she hoped the flower seller would call her back and return the music box, but she didn't.

Estela tried to put the music box out of her mind as she thought about what she could bring to Swap Meet next week. Buyers liked low prices. Maybe she could sell some of her old games or stuffed animals. When she got home, she'd search her room for other things buyers might want. She'd also have to ask Papa if she could come back next week.

Later in the day, near closing time, Papa suddenly called out, "Estela, your friend is here."

Estela turned around. There was the flower seller.

"Since we are at Swap Meet," the woman said, "it is only fair that we swap." She handed Estela a bag. "Good-bye for now, little one," the flower seller said, and hurried off.

Estela looked inside. "The *falda!*" she exclaimed.

Estela pulled the skirt out of the bag and put it on over her clothes. She twirled round and round, picturing herself dancing with the Ballet Folklórico.

"May I come back with you next week, Papa?" Estela asked, thinking of the money she still needed to earn.

"Of course, Estela. It looks like you know how to swap," Papa said.

"Yes," said Estela. "But now I need to learn how to sell."